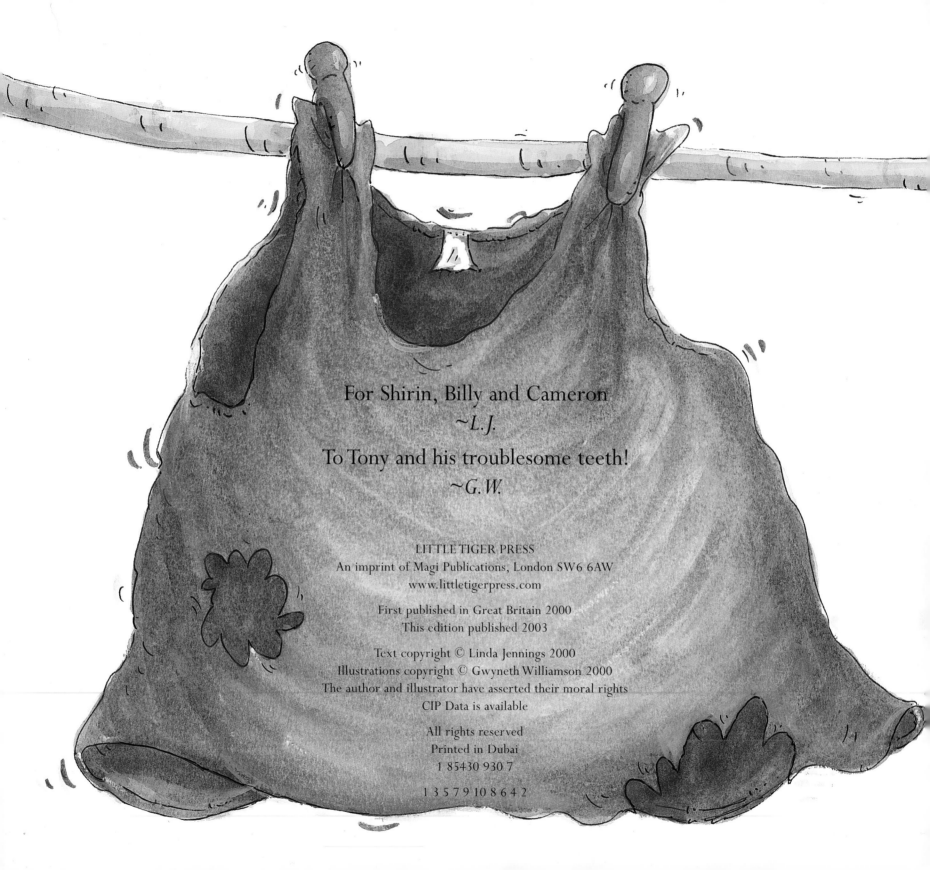

For Shirin, Billy and Cameron
~L.J.

To Tony and his troublesome teeth!
~G.W.

LITTLE TIGER PRESS
An imprint of Magi Publications, London SW6 6AW
www.littletigerpress.com

First published in Great Britain 2000
This edition published 2003

Text copyright © Linda Jennings 2000
Illustrations copyright © Gwyneth Williamson 2000
The author and illustrator have asserted their moral rights
CIP Data is available

Printed in Dubai
1 85430 930 7

1 3 5 7 9 10 8 6 4 2

Titus's Troublesome Tooth

Linda Jennings and Gwyneth Williamson

LITTLE TIGER PRESS

Titus the Goat ate everything.
He ate carrots and cabbages.

He ate dandelions and dockleaves.

He ate prickly, tickly thistles . . .

and he even ate Farmer
Harry's underwear off
the washing line!

Titus absolutely
loved eating —
until one day . . .

he woke up with
a terrible pain.

He didn't want
his breakfast . . .

and he didn't want to munch
and crunch the apples
in the orchard.

He wasn't even tempted to
nibble at Mrs. Harry's nightdress.
Titus felt as miserable as . . .

well, as miserable as a goat with toothache!
He was a very grouchy, grumbly goat indeed.

"That's a troublesome tooth," said Derry
the Donkey. "Open your mouth and I'll
pull it out with my big, strong teeth."

Titus shook from his
horns to the tip of his tail.
"Ooh-er, no thanks," he bleated.
He ran and ran and grouched
and grumbled . . .

until he reached the barnyard.

"That's a troublesome tooth," said Sadie
the Hen. "Open your mouth and I'll peck
it out with my nice, sharp beak."
Titus quivered on all four hooves.
"Ooh-er, no thanks," he cried.
Titus ran and ran and grouched
and grumbled . . .

until he reached the barn. "That's a troublesome tooth," said Polly the Cat. "Open your mouth and I'll scratch it out with my long, shiny claws."

Titus trembled from his white beard to his furry bottom. "Ooh-er, no thanks," he shouted.

Titus ran and ran and grouched and grumbled . . .

until he reached
the meadow.
"That's a troublesome
tooth," said Basil the Bull. "Open your mouth and I'll
butt it out with my hard, curly horns."

All Titus's teeth chattered and
rattled — even the bad one!
"Ooh-er, no thanks," he sobbed.
Titus ran and ran and grouched
and grumbled . . .

until he reached the duck pond.

"That's a troublesome tooth," said Daphne the
Duck. "Open your mouth and I'll tug it out with
some duckweed."

Titus shook so much that he nearly fell into the water.

"Ooh-er, no thanks," he yelled.

Titus ran and ran and grouched and grumbled . . .

until he found himself right
back in the barnyard again.
"Don't worry," said Sadie the Hen.

"Farmer Harry will get rid of that troublesome tooth for you, because he's called the Vet!"

"The Vet!"

shouted Titus.

He quivered and he shivered,
he trembled and he shook.
His teeth rattled and
chattered — even the
bad one.
"No way do I want *the Vet!*"

Titus ran and ran

and grouched

and grumbled until . . .

Titus bashed his head against the fence . . .

CRASH

and the troublesome
tooth fell out at last!